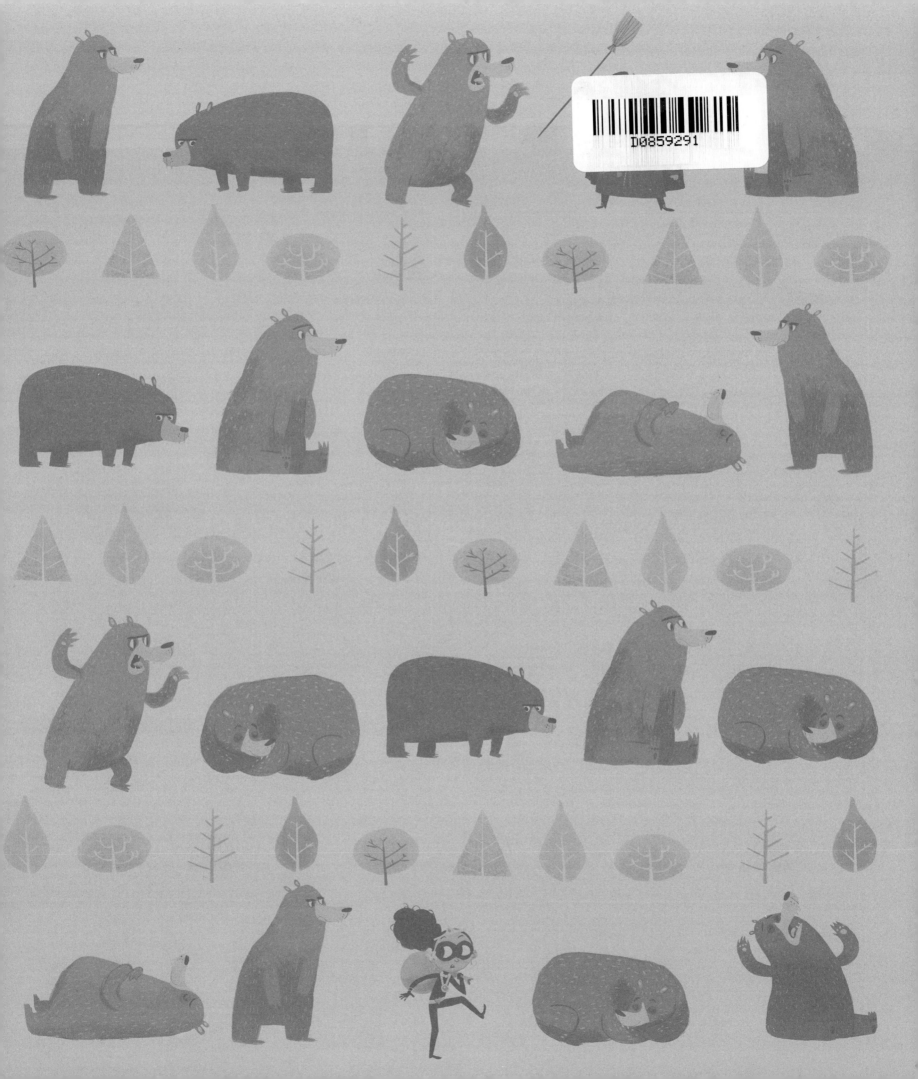

The Prince and the Witch and the Thief and the Bears

For Rose and Amelie ~ A.C.

For Grace ~ J.T.

First American Edition 2019 * Kane Miller, A Division of EDC Publishing * Text copyright © 2018 Alastair Chisholm * Illustration copyright © 2018 Jez Tuya * The moral rights of the author and illustrator have been asserted. * First published in Great Britain in 2018 by Walker Books Ltd. * All rights reserved. No part of this book may be reproduced, transmitted, broadcast or stored in an information retrieval system in any form or by any means, graphic, electronic or mechanical, including photocopying, taping and recording, without prior written permission from the publisher. * For information contact: Kane Miller, A Division of EDC Publishing, P.O. Box 470663, Tulsa, OK 74147-0663 * Library of Congress Control Number: 2018949389 Printed and bound in China

ISBN: 978-1-61067-849-0 * 1 2 3 4 5 6 7 8 9 10 * www.kanemiller.com

The Prince and the Witch and the Thief and the Bears

ALASTAIR CHISHOLM

illustrated by JEZ TUYA

Kane Miller

A DIVISION OF EDC PUBLISHING

"**W**hat kind of story shall we have tonight?"
asked Dad, as he tucked Jamie into bed
one evening.
"A made-up one!" said Jamie.
"With a Prince and a bear!
And a witch. And more bears!"
"All right," said Dad. "Why not?"

"This," said Dad, "is a story called ...

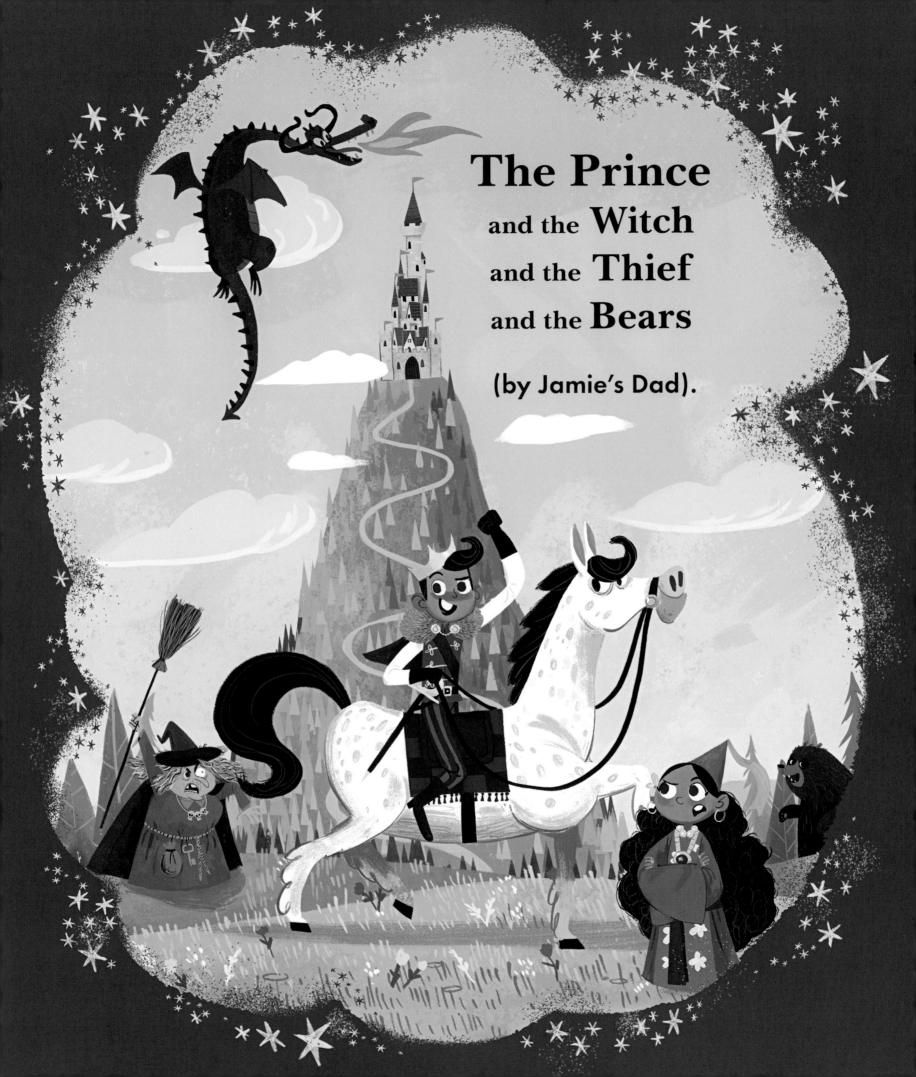

The Prince
and the Witch
and the Thief
and the Bears

(by Jamie's Dad).

Once upon a time," said Dad, "there lived a valiant Prince. He was a brave and noble Prince, and he lived in a far-off kingdom, where he—"

"How far off?" asked Jamie.

"What?" asked Dad.
"How far off was the kingdom?"
"The kingdom," said Dad, "was …

far, far away on the top of the highest mountain
in the world, Mount ReeliReeliTol,
where fierce bears and dragons
and wolves prowl."

"How fierce were the bears?" asked Jamie.

"Very fierce," said Dad. "Enormous and shaggy,
with thick matted hair and vicious claws
as big as your *head*."

"So how did the Prince get past the bears, then?"
"He climbed down the cliff side,
where the bears
couldn't reach,"
said Dad.

"Wow," said Jamie. "With his horse as well?"

"Er ... ye-es," said Dad.

"He ... carried his horse
on his back."

"Wow."

"He was very strong,"
said Dad.

"So," said Dad, "there was this Prince, and he was very brave, and one day he set off to rescue a beautiful Princess—"

"Why couldn't the Princess rescue the Prince?" complained Jamie. "Mom says Princesses in stories are *rubbish*."

"Well, in this story it's the Prince."

"I want it to be the Princess," said Jamie.

"All right," replied Dad. "Why not?
The very brave *Princess* set off—"

"No actually I want the Prince," said Jamie.
"The PRINCE," exclaimed Dad,
"set off to rescue the Princess!

The Princess was a prisoner
in a dark tower at the edge of the forest.
She was being held there by her
wicked aunt who was really
a Witch with an Evil Eye."

"How evil?"

"So evil that it could turn you … into *stone*," said Dad.

"Or jello?" asked Jamie.

"No, stone."

"But maybe jello sometimes?"

"Well, ok, yes, sometimes," said Dad.

"Good," said Jamie. "I like jello."

Before

After

Before

After

Before

After

Before

After

"The Witch had locked the Princess up in the tower—"
"Why did she do that?"

"She did it ... to set a trap for the Prince. The Witch *hated*
the Prince because he'd laughed at her only friend ...

a tiny green frog,
just as big as your thumb,
who lived in the folds of the Witch's cloak.

And so it was that the Prince rode for many miles
until he reached the tower, a terrible,
awful place called Castle …
Castle…"

"*Broccoli,*" said Jamie, darkly.
"Castle Broccoli."
"I don't like broccoli,"
muttered Jamie.

"At the top of the disgusting, *hideous* Castle Broccoli, the Prince looked for the Princess ... but before he could rescue her—"

"The Witch caught him!"
shouted Jamie.
"The Witch caught him,"
agreed Dad.

"And they had a fight!"
shouted Jamie.
"And they had a fight,"
agreed Dad.

"Because the Witch was really a *Ninja!*" said Jamie. "Because the Witch was really ... a Ninja? Yes! *Exactly!*" said Dad.

"The Witch, *who was really a Ninja,* attacked the Prince with a mighty leaping kick…

But he dodged
and she flew over
the castle walls
and . . .
and . . ."

"And?"

"And was eaten by the bears!" said Dad dramatically.

"Oh," said Jamie.

Dad looked down.

"What's wrong?" he asked.

"I *liked* the Witch," said Jaime. "She was a Ninja and she had an Evil Eye and a frog. And anyway, it was all the silly Prince's fault for laughing. And she never got to turn anyone into jello..."

"Hmmm," said Dad. "Right."

"The Witch was eaten by the bears..." he said.

"Or so it seemed!"

But at the last minute, the *Princess*, who was secretly a famous jewel thief called *Fingers Malloy* …

picked the lock of her cell …

ran to the wall, threw
down a grappling rope ...

and caught the Witch!"
"Yay!"

"But then, the tiny frog fell out of the Witch's cloak!"

"Oh no!" said Jamie.

"Oh no!" said the Prince (said Dad).

"The Witch grabbed the frog, and the Princess
and the Prince *heaved* her back up—"

"And the horse helped!" said Jamie.

"And the horse helped, of course!" said Dad.

"Together they pulled the Witch and her frog back up to the top of the castle and to safety."

"Hurray!"

"The Witch was so grateful to them for rescuing her frog
that she said sorry for capturing the Princess.
And the Prince said sorry to the Witch
for laughing at her frog, and then the Prince
and the Princess (who was secretly
the jewel thief *Fingers Malloy*)
set off home for their next adventure.

As night fell and
the stars twinkled over the land of
Mount ReeliReeliTol, the Witch tucked
the frog back into the folds of her cloak,
where it was nice and warm..."

Dad tucked Jamie under the covers.

"How warm?" asked Jamie, blinking sleepily.

"As warm," said Dad, "as a lovely warm bug snuggled up in a rug with a hug from his dad who loves him."

"How much?" murmured Jamie.

"As much," whispered Dad softly,

"as your daddy loves you."

"Daddy?" whispered Jamie.

"Yes?"

"What about the bears?"

"Don't worry," said Dad, "we'll find out about them tomorrow."

And he kissed Jamie good night and left him to dream.